WORLD WAR I LEADERS

ESSENTIAL LIBRARY OF WORLD WAR I

BY AMANDA LANSER

CONTENT CONSULTANT

JASON MYERS, PHD
INDEPENDENT SCHOLAR

Essential Library

An Imprint of Abdo Publishing
abdopublishing.com

abdopublishing.com

Published by Abdo Publishing, a division of ABDO, PO Box 398166, Minneapolis, Minnesota 55439.

Printed in the United States of America, North Mankato, Minnesota

092015
012016

THIS BOOK CONTAINS
RECYCLED MATERIALS

Cover Photos: Bettmann/Corbis/AP Images, left, right
Interior Photos: Bettmann/Corbis/AP Images, 1 (left), 1 (right); Harris & Ewing/Library of Congress, 4, 50, 99 (top); Ernst Sandau, 6; Everett Historical/Shutterstock Images, 9, 11, 58, 88; Bain News Service/Library of Congress, 14, 20, 28, 55, 70, 76, 78, 98 (top), 99 (bottom); World History Archive/Newscom, 17, 27, 37, 40, 48, 73, 75, 82; Bettmann/Corbis, 25, 68; George Shuklin, 30; Le Patriote Illustré, 32; Library of Congress, 39, 64, 98 (bottom); Cay Jacob Arthur Renard, 43; Agence Rol, 46; AP Images, 53; Charles L. Franck/War Department, 61; Edward N. Jackson/US Army Signal Corps, 63; Hulton-Deutsch Collection/Corbis, 85; Public Domain, 86, 91; Red Line Editorial, 92, 93; Hermann Rex, 94

Editor: Jenna Gleisner
Series Designer: Kelsey Oseid and Maggie Villaume

CONTENTS

CHAPTER 1 SLOUCHING TOWARD WAR 4

CHAPTER 2 KAISER WILHELM II 14

CHAPTER 3 CZAR NICHOLAS II 28

CHAPTER 4 KING VICTOR EMMANUEL III 40

CHAPTER 5 PRESIDENT WOODROW WILSON 50

CHAPTER 6 PRIME MINISTER DAVID LLOYD GEORGE 64

CHAPTER 7 PREMIER GEORGES CLEMENCEAU 76

CHAPTER 8 THE ELEVENTH HOUR 88

Czar Nicholas II of Russia was greatly offended by Austria-Hungary and Germany's actions, later fighting against the countries.

CHAPTER 1

SLOUCHING TOWARD WAR

"It is quite true that the form and method of Germany's action—I mean towards us—has simply been brutal and we won't forget it," Czar Nicholas II of Russia penned to his mother.[1] He was reacting to Austria-Hungary's annexation of Bosnia in October 1908. An ally of Germany, Austria-Hungary's move threatened Russia's influence over the region known as the Balkans. Nicholas placed blame for Austria-Hungary's aggression on the shoulders of Germany and its leader, Kaiser Wilhelm II. Wilhelm also happened to be Nicholas's third cousin.

The annexation caused outrage in Russia and the Balkan nation of Serbia, which Russia had sworn to protect. Serbia, with Russia's

support, demanded Austria-Hungary give Serbia a part of Bosnia. But when Austria-Hungary, backed by its ally, Germany, threatened war, Serbia and Russia were forced to back off. Nicholas would not forget the way Germany and its ally had treated him and his country. When the world ignited into war in August 1914, Nicholas would enter the war on the side of his first cousin, King George V of the United Kingdom.

A FAMILY AFFAIR

With the exception of France, which was a republic, all European nations had monarchs. Though the monarchs had varying degrees of political and military power, they all had symbolic importance

Nicholas, *left*, and his first cousin King George V, *right*

and influenced how their countries acted on the world stage.

Three of these monarchs were also related. Wilhelm of Germany and George of the United Kingdom were first cousins, both grandsons of British Queen Victoria. George and Nicholas of Russia were also first cousins. Nicholas's wife was a granddaughter of Queen Victoria. Though related, these monarchs found themselves at odds in World War I. Wilhelm II is known to have said that if Queen Victoria had been alive, she would never have allowed her grandchildren to go to war against each other.

ALL MONARCHS WERE NOT EQUAL

Though Nicholas II, George V, and Wilhelm II were all monarchs, they did not have the same powers. As czar of Russia, Nicholas II had nearly complete control of the government and military. He could create policies and give orders to troops himself. As king of the United Kingdom, George V had very limited powers. The British Parliament and constitution put the ability to lead the government and military in the hands of politicians and the law. As emperor of Germany, Wilhelm II's power fell somewhere between that of Nicholas II and George V.

WAR BEGINS

The family relationships between the monarchs of the major European powers could not prevent the outbreak of World War I. Austria-Hungary's annexation of Bosnia stirred anti-Austrian sentiment in the Balkans. On June 28, 1914, seven Serbian nationalists traveled to Sarajevo, the capital of Bosnia. The heir to the throne of Austria-Hungary, Archduke Franz Ferdinand, was visiting the city. The nationalists planned to assassinate the archduke. One of them, Gavrilo Princip, shot and killed the archduke and his wife, Sophie.

It took Austria-Hungary a month to decide how to react to the assassination. On July 28, 1914, it declared war against Serbia. As an ally of Serbia, Russia mobilized its military to defend it. But Russia was also an ally of France, which borders Germany. And Germany was an ally of Austria-Hungary. Threatened by France in the west and by Russia in the east, Germany declared war on Russia and on France and neutral Belgium a few days later. Austria-Hungary in turn declared war on Russia. World War I had begun.

Not all nations were pulled into the conflict at its outbreak. Belgium, which lay between Germany and France, attempted to remain neutral at the onset of the war. But its neutrality was quickly violated by Germany, which hoped to march through the country into France. The United Kingdom declared war on Germany for its invasion of Belgium. King Victor Emmanuel III of Italy, which bordered Austria-Hungary, declared neutrality. But Italy too would be pulled into the

TIMELINE OF WAR DECLARATIONS

- Austria-Hungary (Emperor Franz Joseph) declares war on Serbia on July 28, 1914.
- Germany (Kaiser Wilhelm II) declares war on Russia on August 1, 1914.
- Germany (Kaiser Wilhelm II) declares war on France on August 3, 1914.
- Germany (Kaiser Wilhelm II) declares war on Belgium on August 4, 1914.
- United Kingdom (King George V) declares war on Germany on August 4, 1914.
- Austria-Hungary (Emperor Franz Joseph) declares war on Russia on August 6, 1914.

Princip, *second from right*, was arrested for his role in the assassination of Archduke Franz Ferdinand.

conflict in 1915. Across the Atlantic Ocean, President Woodrow Wilson and the United States observed the events in Europe. Reluctant to get the United States involved in a foreign war, Wilson declared US neutrality in August 1914, shortly after the war began.

The initial conflicts along Germany's western border with France and Belgium were known collectively as the battle of the Frontiers. The skirmishes occurred between August 14 and September 6 in the French towns of Mulhouse, Charleroi, and Mons, and the Ardennes and Lorraine regions. Together, the conflicts were the largest battle of World War I and possibly the largest battle in human history. Two million troops fought in the battle of the Frontiers.[2]

The battle of the Frontiers ended on September 6, when the French started fighting the Germans back in the battle of the Marne. French troops were able

MISCALCULATING BELGIUM

At the outbreak of World War I, Belgium was a neutral country. Lying between northeast France and northwest Germany, it hoped to stay out of the war. But Germany planned to march through Belgium to invade France and quickly capture Paris. The day before it declared war on France, Germany wrote to Belgium. It gave the country a choice: allow German troops to march through Belgium without resistance or face occupation by German troops. Germany hoped Belgium would allow the passage. But Belgium refused, warning Germany that if it marched on Belgium, it would be violating international law. Germany invaded Belgium the next day, with two major consequences: Germany now had to fight Belgian troops all the way through Belgium to France. In addition, the United Kingdom entered the war against Germany in defense of Belgium's neutrality.

British troops prepare to resist German advances during the battle of Charleroi on August 21, 1914.

to beat back the German armies, saving Paris from capture. However, Germany retained control of much of northeast France, including France's sources of coal, steel, and iron. The leaders of Europe had embroiled the continent in a war that would last four years and affect the lives of millions.

FOUR YEARS OF WAR

When World War I began in July 1914, many believed the conflict would be over by Christmas. But that hope was not to become reality. Between February and December 1916, the longest, most intense battle in history to that point occurred in the woods of Verdun, France. When it was over, virtually no land had been ceded or gained, and 300,000 soldiers lost their lives.[3] That same year, British and French troops attacked the Germans along the Somme River in France. Its first day, July 1, was the single bloodiest day in British military history with 20,000 British troops killed and more than 40,000 wounded.[4] Similar to Verdun, the battle of the Somme did not gain land for either side but cost hundreds of thousands in casualties. In the wake of the battles of Verdun and the Somme, David Lloyd George became prime minister of the United Kingdom in December 1916. He would lead the country until 1922.

THE WAR OF ATTRITION

The battle of Verdun was the conflict that solidified World War I as a war of attrition. Instead of a swift, decisive victory for either side, the battle and the war would end once one side had lost the manpower and supplies to carry on fighting. By the end of fighting in Verdun in December 1916, virtually no land was gained for either side despite the high rate of casualties.

The new year did not bring an end to the conflict. In February 1917, Germany renewed its policy of unrestricted submarine warfare against ships from all nations in the waters around the United Kingdom. It was the last straw for President Wilson, who had struggled to keep the United States neutral despite pressure at home and abroad to enter the war. On April 6, he asked Congress to declare war against Germany. By the fall, US troops were fighting overseas. This was music to the ears of Georges Clemenceau, who was elected as the premier of France in November 1917.

Meanwhile, Czar Nicholas II faced civil unrest in Russia. He had declared himself supreme commander of the military in 1915, and his government had fallen into disarray while he was at the front. He was forced to abdicate the throne on March 15, 1917. After months of instability, a political group called the Bolsheviks took control of Russia and withdrew the country from the war.

By the spring of 1918, Wilhelm's military advisers had started a series of five offensives they hoped would end the war. These offenses ceased in June, when Allied forces, now under the central command of French general Ferdinand Foch, began offensives of their own. By October, Germany's defeat was clearly on the horizon. Wilhelm abdicated the throne just days before Germany signed an armistice with the Allies on November 11, 1918, ending World War I.

Wilhelm led Germany into World War I.

CHAPTER 2

KAISER WILHELM II

Kaiser Wilhelm II was born on January 27, 1859, in Potsdam, Germany, outside Berlin. Wilhelm's full name was Friedrich Wilhelm Viktor Albert. He was the oldest child of Crown Prince Frederick of Prussia and Victoria, daughter of Queen Victoria of the United Kingdom. His close ties to the United Kingdom, Austria-Hungary, and Russia influenced Wilhelm's decisions leading up to the war.

After serving in the German military as a young man, Wilhelm became the emperor of Germany in 1888. He was only 29 years old. His father was unable to rule because he was gravely ill. As kaiser, or emperor, Wilhelm did not have total control of the German government. He could not make laws and command the military himself but chose the people who could. He had the power to appoint the chancellor, or leader of the civil government, and the leaders of the army and navy. One of his first decisions was to dismiss Chancellor Otto von Bismarck. Bismarck helped found the German empire in 1871 and focused his efforts as chancellor on expanding Germany's foreign influence. Years of Bismarck's political dealings with France made the nation an enemy of Germany. His replacement, Leo von Caprivi, decided not to renew a treaty Bismarck arranged with Russia. The agreement had prevented France from forming an alliance with Russia. Wilhelm assumed France, Germany's neighbor to the west, would not create an alliance with Russia. But Wilhelm had misread the situation. In 1894, Russia and France secretly signed the Dual Alliance. Russia wanted France's support if Russia and Austria-Hungary went to war. Austria-Hungary was an empire in central Europe that bordered Russia and Germany. France wanted Russia's support in a war against Germany. If Germany declared war against Russia, France would come to Russia's defense.

SETTING THE STAGE FOR WAR

In the 26 years between becoming kaiser in 1888 and the start of World War I in 1914, Wilhelm focused his rule on trying to expand Germany's international influence. Though he had little power to create foreign policy, Wilhelm took an intense interest in Germany's dealings with other nations. He helped decide who would serve as Germany's ambassadors in foreign countries.

Wilhelm, *left*, in 1910 with King George V, *right*, believed his meetings, telegrams, and letters with other rulers could expand Germany's influence.

But in his interactions with other rulers, Wilhelm often presented ideas for diplomacy that caused other nations—and Wilhelm's own advisers—to distrust him. Historians describe Wilhelm as a man who pursued new ideas or tactics with vigor but soon grew bored and moved on to the next new idea. His behavior made it difficult for other nations to know Germany's true intentions. In one meeting with the United States, Wilhelm joked about asking France to give territory to Germany to make room for Germany's growing population. The United States included his remark in its records of diplomacy with Germany, unsure of whether Wilhelm was joking or serious.

THE WITHERED ARM

Due to complications during his birth, Wilhelm had no use of his left arm. He tried to conceal his paralyzed arm his entire life. Many historians believe he overcompensated for his disability during his reign. He did not want Germany—or himself—to seem weak or powerless. This may explain his desire for a strong military and aggression toward other nations.

Wilhelm's approach to foreign policy focused primarily on Germany's military might, especially that of its navy. This threatened the United Kingdom, an island nation with the strongest navy in the world. Wilhelm proposed invading the Middle East and making it a German colony. During a conflict in China in 1900, he thought Germany should send troops to secure part of the nation for Germany. He asked the staff of the navy to create plans to invade Puerto Rico, Cuba, and New York. But these invasions were never seriously pursued. Wilhelm tempered his aggressive tone and intentions when the threat of actual war appeared.

Because of Wilhelm's unpredictability, Germany's political leaders tried to limit his involvement in important foreign decisions. This irritated Wilhelm, but it meant his more unrealistic ideas never became foreign policy. But by the summer of 1914, Wilhelm's interactions with other rulers and his bravado would put Germany in a dire situation.

A MISSTEP LEADS TO WAR

In mid-July 1914, Wilhelm was on his yearly summer cruise in Scandinavia. On July 14, he stopped in Norway to reply to a note from Austria-Hungary. The country and its emperor, Franz Joseph, sought Germany's help in deciding how to react to the assassination of Archduke Franz Ferdinand. The two nations had been allies since 1879. They promised to defend each other if either nation was attacked by Russia, an ally of Serbia.

Though he made no reference to war in his response, Wilhelm was firm. He told Austria-Hungary to take a hard stance against Serbia. He called the assassins "crazed fanatics" and said it was the duty of Austria-Hungary to defend its monarchy.[1] The rest of his letter offered various solutions to the impending conflict between Serbia and Austria-Hungary.

EMPEROR FRANZ JOSEPH

1830–1916

Franz Joseph was the emperor of Austria-Hungary when World War I began. He was the successor and nephew of Emperor Ferdinand of Austria, who had no children. Franz Joseph was named emperor in 1848 when he was just 18. Franz Joseph himself met with Wilhelm II and Czar Nicholas II of Russia, helping maintain peace and friendliness between the countries between the 1870s and the years leading to World War I. But his advisers encouraged Franz Joseph to expand Austria-Hungary's influence in the Balkans, which brought the empire into conflict with Germany and Russia. His foreign minister persuaded him to declare war against Serbia in the aftermath of the death of Archduke Franz Ferdinand, starting the war.

The next day, Austria-Hungary sent a response. It planned to issue Serbia an ultimatum: either allow Austria-Hungary to control the investigation of the assassination in Sarajevo and eliminate the anti-Austrian terrorists and propaganda or go to war. Austria-Hungary warned Wilhelm to mobilize Germany's military in case the ultimatum failed. It would send its conditions to Serbia on July 23 and give the country 48 hours to reply.

Despite the firm tone of the ultimatum, Wilhelm believed war was unlikely. He told his secretary of foreign affairs, "Any reason for war has now been eliminated."[2] But Austria-Hungary intended to use the ultimatum as a reason to go to war. It believed Serbia would not agree to all of its terms.

Serbia knew Austria-Hungary was preparing for war and suspected Germany was, too. But it also felt Austria-Hungary's demand to control the investigation undermined its independence. On the afternoon of July 25, Serbia sent its response to Austria-Hungary, but not before mobilizing its army. Serbia agreed to stomp out the terrorists and end the propaganda, but it would not allow Austria-Hungary to investigate the assassination. On July 28, Austria-Hungary declared war on Serbia.

STATE OF IMMINENT DANGER OF WAR

The result of the ultimatum greatly surprised Wilhelm and threw Germany's political and military leaders into a frenzy. On July 29, reports came in describing the movement of Russia's military. German Minister of War Erich von Falkenhayn pled with Wilhelm to declare a State of Imminent Danger of War (SIDW). It would show Germany's intent to defend itself if Russia continued mobilizing its troops. But Chief of General Staff Helmuth von Moltke and Chancellor Bethmann Hollweg disagreed. They wanted Wilhelm to fortify the troops guarding Germany's transportation infrastructure. Doing so would increase Germany's defenses while not implying Germany intended to go to war.

At first, Wilhelm sided with Moltke and Hollweg. But two days later, Russia fully mobilized its military to defend Serbia. Wilhelm now had no choice. Despite his tendency to back down when war was imminent, he had to issue an SIDW and mobilize Germany's troops. The next day, Germany formally declared war on Russia.

Declaring war on Russia had serious consequences. Russia was allied with France, and France was allied with the United Kingdom. Wilhelm hoped the United Kingdom would not enter the war in France's defense if France declared war on Germany to support Russia. Due to conversations held between British and German diplomats, Wilhelm believed the United Kingdom would remain neutral if France kept out of the conflict. But just in case France declared war against Germany, Wilhelm ordered his generals to mobilize troops toward France while waiting to see how the United Kingdom responded.

Waiting for the British response to Germany's military mobilization created hours of angst for Wilhelm and his advisers. Finally, word arrived from a British diplomat: if Germany did not invade France, the United Kingdom would not enter the war and would guarantee that France would not attack Germany. Despite objections from Moltke, Wilhelm halted any further troop movements toward France. He sent a telegram to British King George V accepting his terms. But there had been a misunderstanding. The United Kingdom had never intended to make such a proposal. Germany moved forward with the mobilization of its troops. Already at war with Russia, Germany declared war on France and neutral Belgium, through which it wished to invade France, on August 3. France and Belgium reciprocated hours

THE GERMAN STEAM ROLLER

Germany invaded Belgium on August 5, and in just two weeks, Belgian troops were overwhelmed by the German advance. The German army marched through Belgium's capitol, Brussels, on August 20. US reporter Richard Harding Davis was there to witness the march. He noted the force with which Germany invaded, comparing it to that of a steam roller:

> *"The boulevards fell suddenly empty," he recalled. "At eleven o'clock . . . down the Boulevard Waterloo came the advance-guard of the German army. It consisted of three men, a captain and two privates on bicycles. . . . Behind them, so close upon each other that to cross from one sidewalk to the other was not possible, came the [cavalry], infantry, and the guns. For two hours I watched them, and then, bored . . . returned to the hotel. . . . All through the night . . . in my sleep I could hear the steady roar of the passing army. . . . This was a machine, endless, tireless, with . . . the brute power of a steam roller. And for three days and three nights through Brussels it roared and rumbled, a cataract of molten lead."*[3]

later. The next day, the United Kingdom declared war on Germany in response to its invasion of neutral Belgium and its ally, France.

A KAISER AT WAR

Despite his position as emperor of Germany, Wilhelm's most significant contributions during World War I were his actions before the war. He was nominally the commander in chief of the German military, but he rarely went against the wishes of his generals. He did not oversee the daily operations of the war. Wilhelm did, however, tour the front lines and give out medals to deserving servicemen.

He also replaced military leaders who failed to produce German victories. His first change came just over a month into the conflict. Moltke had failed to successfully coordinate the attacks along the French border. Wilhelm replaced Moltke with Falkenhayn. Falkenhayn favored placing more troops

PAUL VON HINDENBURG

By the time Wilhelm appointed Paul von Hindenburg as chief of general staff in 1916, Hindenburg had already served a full military career. He was a veteran of two wars in the 1860s and 1870s and had risen to the rank of general by 1911. When World War I ended, Hindenburg oversaw the withdrawal of German troops from the western front. In 1925, he was elected president of Germany. Hindenburg won reelection in 1932. In 1933, he appointed Adolf Hitler, the leader of the growing Nazi Party, as chancellor. When Hindenburg died a year later, Hitler had amassed enough power to merge the offices of chancellor and president and become dictator of Germany.

Wilhelm, *left*, poses with Hindenburg, *right*, who helped lead Germany's military until the end of the war.

in France rather than Russia. But Falkenhayn's focus on the western front proved unsuccessful, and Wilhelm replaced him on August 29, 1916. Paul von Hindenburg was Wilhelm's next and final choice. Hindenburg, along with his chief aide, Erich Ludendorff, would lead Germany's military. During the war, the two military leaders became more popular in Germany than Wilhelm himself, and effectively ruled Germany as military dictators until the end of World War I.

WILHELM IN EXILE

By October 1918, Germany's defeat in World War I was clear. The country sued for an armistice to end the fighting. The warring nations signed it on November 11, 1918. Wilhelm had abdicated the throne a few days before. He lived the rest of his life in exile in the Netherlands. During that time, France and its allies tried to extradite Wilhelm, or send him away to a different country, to charge him for war crimes. As part of the peace agreement that ended the war, Germany assumed all responsibility for starting the conflict. But the United Kingdom, France, and their allies were never able to extradite Wilhelm. Wilhelm died in the Netherlands on June 4, 1941, while World War II (1939–1945) raged around him.

Wilhelm, *back center*, and the rest of the exiled royal family in the Netherlands in 1925

Nicholas and his wife, Alexandra, *center*, pose with their five children in 1913.

CHAPTER 3

CZAR NICHOLAS II

Czar Nicholas II was born Nikolay Aleksandrovich Romanov on May 18, 1868, in Saint Petersburg, Russia. In 1894, Nicholas took the throne in place of his father, Czar Alexander III. He was just 26. The same year, he married Princess Alexandra of Germany. Nicholas's family had a significant impact on his reign, including the war years.

Of the two monarchs, Alexandra had the more forceful personality. It was at her urging that Nicholas attempted to take an active role in ruling Russia. Though he had military training, Nicholas was by nature a timid person. He preferred to be among his family instead of ruling the nation. Nicholas and Alexandra had four daughters and a son, Alexis. Alexis had a blood disorder called hemophilia, which made it difficult for his body to stop bleeding if he was injured. Throughout the czar's rule, Alexandra would urge Nicholas to seek the help of faith healers, including one named Rasputin. Rasputin gained Alexandra's favor and become a powerful person in the czar's court.

FALSE STEPS IN ASIA

Nicholas's timid nature made the complicated task of ruling even more difficult. He mistrusted his advisers because he felt they were smarter than he was and wanted to take power for themselves. He did not keep a staff of secretaries to handle the details of ruling, such as scheduling and keeping appointments. Instead, he handled many of these finer details himself. This made it difficult for Nicholas to focus on the more important concerns of the large nation.

Alexandra strongly believed in Rasputin's healing powers.

Despite his tendency to be too cautious, in 1904, Nicholas decided it was in Russia's best interests to expand its power and influence in eastern Asia. He believed this region of the world was where Russia's future lay. But many of his advisers warned him the country should focus its attention on the unrest in the Balkans.

Undeterred, Nicholas ordered a series of attacks against Japan over territory in Korea and the Chinese region of Manchuria. But Korea and Manchuria were thousands of miles from Russia's capital, Saint Petersburg. The distance made it difficult to get troops and supplies to the battlefields. Japanese troops defeated Russian forces in a series of battles, turning public opinion against the war and Nicholas. People protested in the streets of Russia's cities. Two months after signing a peace treaty with Japan in August 1905, Nicholas issued the October Manifesto. It established a parliament and constitution in Russia. The Parliament had limited power because it did not control the nation's entire budget or its ministers. Though he no longer had sole responsibility for governing Russia, Nicholas remained a powerful monarch. But the unrest of 1905 would come back to haunt him ten years later during the war.

ALLIANCES TIE NICHOLAS'S HANDS

In 1894, Russia and France formalized their Dual Alliance. It was renewed in 1899 and again in 1912. But Germany and Austria-Hungary physically

Russian forces were no match for the Japanese in 1904.

separated France and Russia. The alliance put Germany and Austria-Hungary in a precarious spot if war broke out with France or Russia.

After signing the Dual Alliance and following Russia's defeat in Asia in 1905, Nicholas turned his attention to the Balkans. Austria-Hungary's annexation of Bosnia in 1908 angered many Russians who had ethnic ties to the Serbian people. After the unrest following the war with Japan, Nicholas and the Russian government saw how exploiting these sympathies and supporting Serbia could improve public support of the government. Nicholas was also worried the unrest in the Balkan states would lead the Ottoman Empire to try to expand into Balkan territory Russia might be interested in acquiring for itself. Russia worked to strengthen its ties to Serbia and supported the country in the Balkan Wars against the Ottoman Empire.

Then, on June 28, 1914, seven young Serbian nationalists arrived in Sarajevo, Bosnia, to assassinate Austro-Hungarian Archduke Franz Ferdinand. Their success tied Nicholas's hands: if Austria-Hungary declared war on Serbia, Russia would have to come to Serbia's aid. On July 29, Russia notified France it was preparing to mobilize its entire military to defend Serbia against Austria-Hungary. Because of the Dual Alliance, the French government would have no choice but to come to Russia's aid by mobilizing its own military. But France knew doing so could provoke Germany into mobilizing its forces against it. The French government urged Russia to be cautious.

THE CZAR WOBBLES

Late on July 29, Russia's military leaders prepared telegrams to set mobilization in motion across the country. But the final order to mobilize had to come from Nicholas. Out of fear of leading Russia into war, he changed his mind about mobilizing all of Russia's troops. Instead, he ordered a partial mobilization. Around midnight, the new order was sent out across the empire. But partially mobilizing troops would make the logistics of mobilizing the entire force at a later date more difficult. His military advisers urged him to reconsider his decision. After nearly an hour of pleading, Nicholas's foreign minister, Sergei Sazonov, convinced the czar general mobilization was in Russia's best interest. Just after 6:00 p.m. on July 30, Nicholas issued the order to mobilize Russia's entire military against Austria-Hungary.

Nicholas's decision sent the German government of his cousin, Wilhelm II, into a frenzy. It issued a SIDW due to the threat its ally, Austria-Hungary, faced from Russia, as well as the threat Germany faced from Russia's ally, France. On August 1, Germany declared war on Russia. Five days later, Austria-Hungary followed suit. Nicholas and Russia were now at war.

THE WILLY-NICKY TELEGRAMS

While Germany and Russia found themselves on opposite sides leading up to World War I, cousins Kaiser Wilhelm and Czar Nicholas continued friendly communication through telegram. Signing their notes "Willy" or "Nicky," the monarchs talked of friendship while their countries prepared for war against each other. When Russia moved to mobilize its troops in July 1914, Wilhelm sent Nicholas a telegram pleading for him to reconsider. After receiving the telegram, the czar changed his mind and ordered partial mobilization. In the end, however, his advisers convinced him general mobilization was necessary.

NICHOLAS AT WAR

In the first year of war, Nicholas found his power strengthened out of necessity.

But it came at the cost of public opinion as the Parliament, which represented the Russian people, lost political power. In September 1915, Nicholas made a decision that would turn low public opinion into public unrest. With no war experience, Nicholas made himself commander in chief of the military. He dismissed the current commander and the war ministers who opposed his decision.

As commander in chief, Nicholas did not try to overrule the tactical decisions of his military leaders. But he did insist on leaving Saint Petersburg for Russia's military headquarters close to the front. This left Alexandra, the czarina, effectively in charge of the country. Alexandra had become very close to the faith healer Rasputin. She dismissed ministers and advisers and replaced them with people Rasputin approved of, most of whom were not competent to govern. This angered politicians and the public.

NICHOLAS ABDICATES

On March 8, 1917, the public had had enough of the policies enacted in Nicholas's absence. Though he had named himself commander in chief, Nicholas had failed to properly equip and prepare Russia's military for war. The army suffered tremendous casualties, more than any other nation in the conflict. At the same time, Nicholas failed to create a plan to feed his people during the war. Food was scarce in the cities. On March 8, 90,000 workers went on strike.[1] Men and women took to the streets of Saint Petersburg. Many troops stationed in the city joined them.

The mob turned violent, and Nicholas finally took action and ordered troops to stop the riots. But his efforts were too little, too late. The Parliament called on Nicholas to abdicate the throne. He did so a few days later on March 15, asking his brother to take his place. But his brother refused. Instead, Parliament established a new temporary government to rule the country. The new government sent Nicholas and his family to western Siberia as punishment. The Russian Revolution was underway.

RASPUTIN

With a long, scraggly beard and penetrating blue eyes, Rasputin was a favorite of Alexandra and Nicholas but hated among the czar's advisers. While maintaining an image as a holy man with the monarchs, Rasputin's behavior outside the court was far from what people expected from a holy man. Though members of the court tried to warn the czar of Rasputin's sexual behavior, Nicholas and Alexandra were blind to it because they believed Rasputin had healed their son. Rasputin continued to hold sway over the monarchs through 1915, when he became Alexandra's personal adviser while Nicholas was at the front.

THE BOLSHEVIKS TAKE CONTROL

During this unrest, the country was still at war with Germany. With Nicholas stripped of power and in exile in Siberia, different political groups tried to gain control of the Russian government. A group of soldiers and workers called the Soviets challenged the temporary government backed by the Parliament. *Soviet* means "council" in Russian. Instead

Looters vandalized Nicholas's office during the Russian Revolution in 1917.

of politicians, it was composed of Russian workers and soldiers. Shortly before Nicholas abdicated, the Soviets had tried to seize power, issuing an order to the military to obey the Soviet government, not the temporary one. The conflict between the Soviets and temporary government continued for six months. The temporary government failed to successfully address low troop morale and stamp out the Soviets. Then, in September 1917, a faction of the Soviets called the Bolsheviks, or "majority," led by Vladimir Lenin, started a campaign to end the war and feed the Russian people. The message resonated with the Russian

PEACE! BREAD! LAND!

During the Russian Revolution, Russian soldiers and workers demanded an end to Russia's involvement in World War I and called for government policies that would provide the Russian people with food and land. The Bolsheviks gained power in the summer and fall of 1917 with the promise of peace, bread, and land to the Russian people. They also demanded the temporary government pull Russia out of World War I, feed Russia's workers, and distribute land held by the ruling class to poor peasants. Meanwhile, the temporary government failed to make the changes the Russian people demanded. The Bolsheviks gradually gained popularity among Russia's workers and soldiers. Once the Bolsheviks took power, their first move was to get Russia out of the war.

people, who were hungry and tired of war. The Bolsheviks gained popularity while the temporary government waned in influence. On October 24, the Bolsheviks staged an overthrow of the government. With little loss of life, the Bolsheviks took over government facilities, establishing Soviet rule in Russia.

Now in control of the government, the Soviets could pull Russia out of World War I. One of the new government's first acts was to propose peace to Germany, Austria-Hungary, Bulgaria, and the Ottoman Empire. An armistice was signed in December 1917, and within a few weeks, Russia's troops started returning home. Russia was out of World War I.

CHAIRMAN VLADIMIR LENIN

1870–1924

Vladimir Lenin founded and chaired the Russian Communist Party, commonly called the Bolsheviks. His work started long before the Bolsheviks took control of Russia in 1917. The czar exiled him to Siberia in 1895 for his revolutionist thinking. After his exile, Lenin traveled to Western Europe. He stayed there for 15 years before returning to Russia in 1917 when the fall of the czar was imminent. Merciless against his competition, Lenin led the Soviets against the temporary government. He led the Soviet government until 1924, when he died after struggling with serious health issues. Lenin was succeeded by Joseph Stalin, who would rule the country as a dictator until his death in 1953.

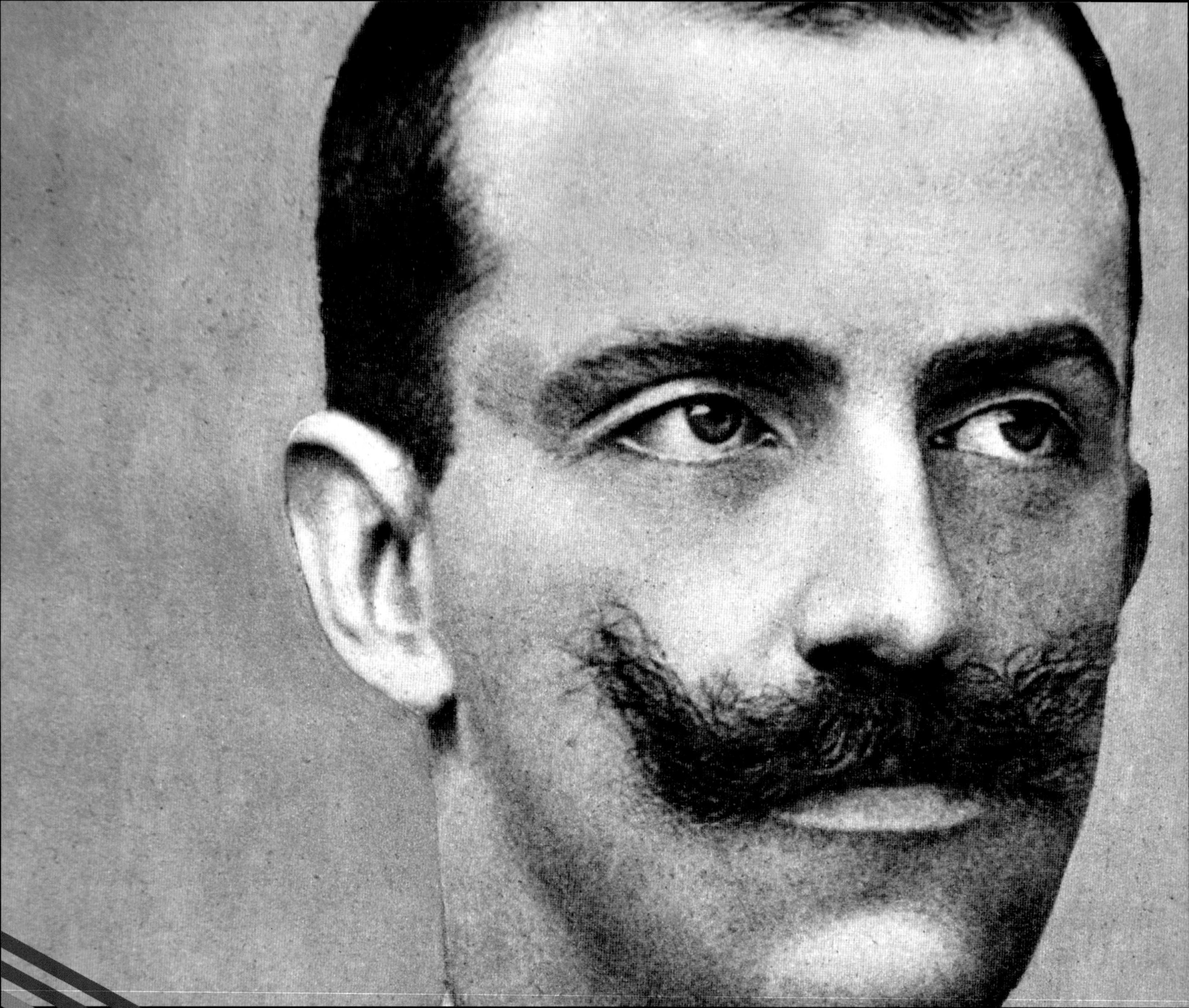

Victor Emmanuel received a military education as a young man.

CHAPTER 4

KING VICTOR EMMANUEL III

King Victor Emmanuel III was born on November 11, 1869, in Naples, Italy. He took the throne in 1900 at age 31 after an anarchist assassinated his father.

As king, Victor Emmanuel cooperated well with the Italian Parliament. He believed his father's government was rarely able to take the initiative, but rather reacted to the social unrest happening in Italy at the time. Victor Emmanuel used his position to support social reforms until the war began. Though not particularly involved in Italy's dealings with other nations, Victor Emmanuel did maintain close relationships with his foreign ministers.

ITALO-TURKISH WAR

Despite his lack of involvement in foreign affairs, Victor Emmanuel took an interest in Italy's military affairs. Similar to Wilhelm II, Victor Emmanuel wished to expand his country's influence in Africa. He used the Agadir Crisis in 1911 as pretense to invade the Turkish provinces of Tripolitania and Cyrenaica (now in modern Libya) on September 28, 1911. He declared Italy's interests in the region had to be protected from the Ottomans.

Victor Emmanuel's decision to invade had implications in North Africa and in the Balkans. At the time, the Ottoman Empire was also facing unrest in its territory in the Balkans. It now had to divide its attention between the Balkans and North Africa. Inspired by Italy's action against the Ottoman Empire, the Balkan states also rose up against the Ottoman Empire. By October 1912, the Ottomans had had enough. A peace treaty ended the Italo-Turkish War and gave Tripolitania and Cyrenaica to Italy. The Ottoman Empire's weakness had been revealed, and the balance of power in North Africa

THE AGADIR CRISIS OF 1911

On July 1, 1911, the *Panther*, a German gunboat, prowled the coastline near the port city of Agadir, Morocco. Wilhelm II sent the boat to intimidate France. France partially controlled Morocco, and Wilhelm had grand plans for expanding Germany's territories in Africa. Wilhelm's move created a panic among his fellow monarchs and brought Europe to the brink of war. It set the stage for the alliances that would become important at the outbreak of World War I (1914–1918).

During what is now coined the Agadir Crisis of 1911, Wilhelm sent the German gunboat *Panther* to Agadir, Morocco, on July 1, 1911, to intimidate the French.

and the Balkans upset. Speaking to how the Italo-Turkish War related to World War I, a former leader of the Serbian foreign ministry was unequivocal. He said, “All subsequent events [after the Italo-Turkish War] are nothing more than the evolution of that first aggression.”[1] The war had given the people in the Balkans the confidence to rise against the Ottomans, destabilizing the region.

SHIFTING ALLIANCES

When Victor Emmanuel took the throne, Italy was an ally of Germany and Austria-Hungary. The countries had signed the Triple Alliance in 1882 and renewed their agreement in 1891, 1902, and 1912. Many wealthy Italians and clergy in Italy thought well of Austria-Hungary before the outbreak of World War I. But public opinion changed over the course of the Triple Alliance. The conservative Italian clergy continued supporting friendly relations with Austria-Hungary. But Italian nationalists wanted to toss out the treaty and confront Austria-Hungary over disputed territory along the Adriatic Sea.

Between 1900 and 1914, Victor Emmanuel tried to bridge the divide in public opinion. In 1900 and 1902, Italy made a secret agreement with France. The agreement canceled out many of the details of the treaty Italy had with Germany and Austria-Hungary. After 1904, the Italian public's good opinion of Austria-Hungary still wavered as the country attempted to expand its influence in the Balkans. The Italians also had their sights on the region. Finally, in October 1909, Victor Emmanuel broke the Triple Alliance. He and Czar Nicholas II of Russia signed a secret agreement to respect each other's territorial interests and not make moves in the Balkans without the other's consent.

WAR BREAKS OUT

Italy's shifting alliances in the decades before the war made it unclear which side Italy should support. When World War I broke out at the end of July 1914, Victor Emmanuel decided the best course of action was to remain neutral. Countries on both sides tried to convince Victor Emmanuel to join their side. Italy's neutrality lasted nearly an entire year. By the spring of 1915, Victor Emmanuel faced increasing pressure from members of the government who wanted Italy to intervene in the war. Pressure mounted after Italy met with the Allies and signed the Treaty of London in April. The treaty guaranteed Italy territory along its border with Austria-Hungary and along the Adriatic Sea. With these assurances, Italy was ready to enter the war. It declared war on Austria-Hungary on May 23, 1915.

Italy's entry into the war opened up a new front. Instead of fighting on the eastern or western fronts, Italian troops fought along Italy's border with Austria-Hungary in the Alps. But Italy was not prepared to wage war against the Austro-Hungarians. Italy had become a unified nation in 1861 and had not yet fully industrialized as its enemies had. It was able to mobilize 1.2 million troops, but had supplies to outfit fewer than 750,000.[2] The Italian front in the Alps quickly turned into an icy stalemate.

POPE BENEDICT XV OPPOSES WAR

Victor Emmanuel was not the only leader in Rome during World War I. Pope Benedict XV led the Catholic Church at the Vatican in Rome during the conflict. He was elected pope just months after the war started and immediately spoke in favor of peace. He called the war "the suicide of Europe" and urged the nations to call a truce over Christmas 1914.[3] However, Victor Emmanuel and other world leaders ignored Benedict's calls for peace. Despite this chilly reception, Benedict continued to call for peace throughout the war years. He drafted a peace proposal in August 1917 and asked to be included at the Paris Peace Conference, but his request was not granted.

The Alps presented difficult terrain and harsh weather conditions for Italian troops.

On October 24, 1917, that stalemate came to a disastrous end for Italy. German and Austro-Hungarian forces initiated an offensive along the Italian line in the Alps. With morale low, the Italians retreated, losing 600,000 troops to surrender or desertion in the process.[4] The retreat and large loss of troops put the Italian military at risk of total collapse.

Due to the structure of the Italian monarchy, it was unclear who the supreme commander of the Italian army was: the chief of the general staff, the minister of war, or the king himself. But after the battle of Caporetto, Victor Emmanuel put his military education to work. Upon the recommendation of French military leader Ferdinand Foch, Victor Emmanuel replaced his chief of general staff, Luigi Cadorna, with Armando Diaz, Cadorna's chief of operations. With new military leadership in place, Victor Emmanuel convinced his fellow Allied leaders Italy could hold the line at the Piave River in northeast Italy. He also appealed to the Italian public for its support and was even able to rally the support of Italian antiwar groups. With the country and military behind him, Victor Emmanuel stayed true to his word. Italian forces held the Piave River despite a series of Austro-Hungarian attacks in 1918. Finally, a year after the defeat at the battle of Caporetto, the Italians led a successful offensive against the Austro-Hungarian forces that led to the defeat of Austria-Hungary in the war and the end to the Austro-Hungarian empire.

THE WHITE WAR

While French, British, Belgian, Russian, and German troops fought in the trenches of the western and eastern fronts, the Italians and Austro-Hungarians found themselves in a vastly different environment. For them, the war was largely fought high up in the Alps. Due to the cold, snowy conditions, this front is known in Italy as the White War. The front in the Alps spanned 250 miles (400 km), much of it above 6,500 feet (2,000 m) in altitude. The troops carved trenches out of ice and used cables to haul supplies and men from the base of the mountains up to the front lines.

ARMANDO DIAZ

1861–1928

Armando Diaz replaced Luigi Cadorna as Italy's chief of staff after the disastrous defeat at the battle of Caporetto. Born in 1861, Diaz received a military education and served in the Italo-Turkish War. In 1914, he was appointed major general of the Italian army. He worked with Cadorna to prepare Italian troops for their entry in the war in 1915. Before Victor Emmanuel named him chief of staff, Diaz served as a division commander and corps commander. As chief of staff, he brought stability to the army and orchestrated the offensive against Austro-Hungarian troops that led to victory at the battle of Vittorio Veneto in 1918. In 1921, he was named *duca della vittoria*, or "duke of victory."

AFTER THE WAR

Though it nearly fell apart under Victor Emmanuel's leadership and staff changes, the Italian military rallied at the end of the war. After the war, a new political ideology known as fascism rose in popularity in Italy. By 1922, it was clear fascists threatened Victor Emmanuel and Parliament. But Victor Emmanuel refused to face the fascists, making it possible for their leader, Benito Mussolini, to rise to power and control the government. Though he still held on to his crown, Victor Emmanuel allowed Mussolini to rule Italy as a dictator for the next two decades. By the end of World War II (1939–1945), public opinion had soured against Victor Emmanuel, who abdicated the throne on May 9, 1946, and died the next year.

THE BATTLE OF VITTORIO VENETO

Though victorious at the Piave River, Diaz was reluctant to conduct an offensive against Austria-Hungary. But Foch urged him to reconsider, especially after it was clear Germany was too preoccupied in France to come to Austria-Hungary's aid. Italian troop morale was high after the success along the Piave River, while Austro-Hungarian morale was low. On October 23, 1918, the Italians attacked in the Alps. Over the next nine days, the Italians pushed the Austro-Hungarians back 15 miles (24 km) until the Austro-Hungarians surrendered on November 2. The Italians lost 38,000 soldiers and took 300,000 Austro-Hungarian prisoners.[5] The major defeat caused turmoil in Austria-Hungary, eventually dismantling the empire.

Woodrow Wilson was a professor and college president before turning to politics and winning the US presidency.

CHAPTER 5

PRESIDENT WOODROW WILSON

Woodrow Wilson was born on December 28, 1856, in Staunton, Virginia. His full name was Thomas Woodrow Wilson. Wilson's father was a Presbyterian minister. The Presbyterian Church played a major role in Wilson's upbringing, as his father moved the family across the country to serve as pastor in different churches. Between 1885 and his election to the presidency in 1912, Wilson was a professor of political science at Bryn Mawr College, Wesleyan University, and Princeton University. In 1902, he became the president of Princeton University. His work there caught the attention of the Democratic Party, which urged him to run for governor of New Jersey in 1910.

As governor, Wilson quickly focused on the upcoming presidential election of 1912. An eloquent and powerful speaker, Wilson knew how to tailor his campaign message to different audiences. Gaining national popularity, Wilson had a unique opportunity in the 1912 presidential election. Instead of two major contenders, there were three: Democratic nominee Wilson, Republican nominee and current president William Howard Taft, and Progressive Party nominee and former president Theodore Roosevelt. Roosevelt, formerly a Republican, broke from the party to run on his own. But doing so split the Republican vote, with some Republicans voting for Taft and others voting for Roosevelt. As a result, Wilson was elected president with less than half of the popular vote.

IRONY OF FATE

At the time Wilson became president, the United States rarely got involved in global affairs. The US public was especially wary of becoming involved in Europe's wars. As early as 1823, the Monroe Doctrine of President James Monroe stated the United States would stay out of Europe's political and military conflicts. Growing instability in Europe was not discussed in the 1912 election and was ignored until the outbreak of war. Just before he took office, Wilson told a friend, "It would be the irony of fate if my administration had to deal chiefly with foreign affairs."[1] Indeed, the war in Europe would become the primary focus of Wilson's administration.

Wilson, *right*, takes the oath of office for his first term as president in Washington, DC, on March 4, 1913.

When Austria-Hungary declared war on Serbia and caused Europe to collapse into conflict in August 1914, Wilson responded immediately with a declaration of neutrality. He believed the United States was not obligated to enter the war on either side. He stated true neutrality required the nation to be fair, friendly, and impartial to everyone, including Germany. This appealed to many German Americans as well as others who feared the United States would enter the war on the side of France and the United Kingdom. However, other Americans were angry with Wilson for keeping the United States out of the war. They believed entry into the war was inevitable and failing to make preparations for war put the United States at risk. But Wilson held fast to his decision to keep the United States neutral. He agreed the nation was not prepared for war, but he also explained there was no need to prepare for war when the United States was at peace with the world's nations. He believed maintaining a professional military went against the US tradition of maintaining a smaller, volunteer force.

JUMP-STARTING AN ECONOMY

When World War I began, the United States was in an economic recession. As European nations pulled their merchant ships into military duty, trade between the United States and Europe dropped significantly. This intensified the economic downturn. Within the first few weeks of the war, prominent US banker J. P. Morgan met with Wilson. France had approached Morgan's bank in hopes of securing a loan to fund its war effort. Morgan believed funding the warring nations in Europe would help bring the United States out of the recession. At first, Wilson disagreed. He was afraid loaning money to one nation would lead to making loans to other nations. He thought this would create a divide among the US people.

But two months later, Wilson changed his mind. Instead of extending loans to countries, he allowed US companies to extend European nations credits for US goods and supplies. Nations could use the credits to receive weapons, food, machinery, and cotton. As Morgan predicted, these credits pulled the US economy out of recession. But though Wilson required credits to be extended

J. P. Morgan helped convince Wilson to fund warring nations.

to nations on either side, over time, more credits were extended to France and the United Kingdom than Germany and its allies. Prior to the war, US banks had strong relationships with British and French banks. And a British blockade of German ports in the North Sea since the beginning of the war made it difficult for supplies to get through to Germany. As a result, France and the United Kingdom received ten times more US credits than Germany and its allies did.

CLOSER TO WAR

Wilson hoped to keep the United States out of World War I, but through 1915 and 1916, developments in the war made it difficult for Wilson to maintain US neutrality. In 1915, Germany announced a policy of unrestricted submarine warfare. All ships, including merchant ships of neutral countries, would be vulnerable to U-boat, or undersea boat, attack. On May 7, a German U-boat sunk a British passenger ship carrying US passengers. The sinking of the *Lusitania* cost more than 120 US lives and forced Wilson to respond.[2] He sent the Germans a strongly worded letter demanding the end of unrestricted submarine warfare. The note worked, and by September 1915 Germany had called off its U-boat attacks.

Despite this success, in December 1915 Wilson called on Congress to increase the size of the US Army, Navy, and merchant marine force. He believed the ships were needed to handle the brisk trade the United States was doing with the warring nations. He also believed a stronger military was necessary to defend US neutrality and peace.

However, by 1917, Germany had increased its aggression toward the United States. In January, the British intercepted a telegram sent from Germany to Mexico. It offered Mexico land in the United States in exchange for joining Germany in the war. Mexico had lost the land in a war with the United States in the 1840s. Then, on February 1, Germany resumed its policy of unrestricted submarine warfare. US merchant ships became targets once more. On April 2, Wilson took to the podium at the US capitol to ask Congress to declare war against Germany. On April 6, 1917, the United States entered World War I.

AMERICAN JINGOES

Not all Americans were content with staying out of World War I. Two of Wilson's most vocal opponents were Theodore Roosevelt and Senator Henry Cabot Lodge. Both men were jingoes, or people who believed the United States should enter the war in the name of patriotism. Roosevelt worried war was inevitable and Wilson's policy of neutrality would leave the nation vulnerable. Roosevelt and Lodge believed the nation was obligated to enter the war after the loss of US lives in the sinking of the *Lusitania*.

AMERICA AT WAR

When the United States declared war on Germany, it was only the fourth time in history the nation had declared war on another country. The last time was the Spanish-American War in 1898. Immediately, Wilson called on Congress to strengthen the military. On April 6,

Wilson addressed the US Congress on April 2, 1917.

only 300,000 men served in the US military.[3] On May 18, Congress passed the Selective Service Act. It created a national draft that selected men to serve in the military. In 18 months, more than 25 million men would be registered for the draft.[4] Approximately 4.36 million would serve.[5] Wilson also asked Congress to change national transportation policy to make it easier to transport war materials across the country. And he put the nation's railroads under federal control. This made it more efficient for troops and supplies to cross the country by rail.

COMMITTEE ON PUBLIC INFORMATION

The US Committee on Public Information helped shape US opinion on World War I after the United States entered the conflict. Though it did not censor information from Europe, it did control how information was presented. Propaganda posters, pamphlets, and films appealed to Americans' patriotism while calling the Germans barbaric. One notable poster featured a pointing Uncle Sam with the caption, "I want YOU for US Army."

Wilson also established a number of agencies to centralize the nation's war efforts. The Council of National Defense included a committee of cabinet secretaries, including the secretaries of the interior, labor, war, and commerce. It also included a commission of business and other leaders, including labor leader Samuel Gompers and the president of Sears department stores. The commission was tasked with managing the logistics of getting supplies to US troops in Europe.

While he sent soldiers overseas to fight, Wilson also enlisted the help of men, women, and children at home. Though the United States did not adopt a formal rationing policy, Wilson asked women to observe "meatless Mondays" and "wheatless Wednesdays" so more food could go to the troops. He also started a very successful war bond campaign. The US public purchased the bonds, called Liberty Loans, to help fund the war effort. Four campaigns raised $17 billion by the end of the war.[6]

By June 1918, there were 1.5 million US troops in France.[7] Wilson made it clear to the leaders of the United Kingdom and France that US troops were not replacements for their European counterparts, but a force in their own right. They would fight together as US units rather than serve in French or British units. US troops proved themselves throughout the month of June in the battle of Belleau Wood, which marked the end of the last major German offensive.

WILSON PLANS FOR PEACE

While US forces served overseas, Wilson focused his efforts on drafting a plan for peace after the war ended. In January 1918, he organized his ideas into 14 main points. Among them was a call to end secret agreements in favor of open and public diplomacy between nations. Wilson also wished for nations to reduce the size of their armies to a force just large enough for self-defense. He called for the autonomy of Russia, Belgium, France, Austria-Hungary, the Ottoman Empire, and the Balkan states of Serbia, Romania, and Montenegro. Wilson also wished to establish Poland as a new and free nation. The idea that these nations had the right to rule themselves was a big change in the imperial attitude European monarchs had before the war. The fourteenth point was the one Wilson

At this Liberty Loan drive in New Orleans, Louisiana, in 1918, US citizens were urged to conserve and ration food.

considered most important. It called for the creation of a League of Nations that would mutually guarantee the independence and territories of member nations. An attack on one nation in the league would be an attack on all league nations.

Wilson took his Fourteen Points with him to the Paris Peace Conference. In negotiations with David Lloyd George and Georges Clemenceau, Wilson used his speaking and diplomacy skills to push for the creation of the League of Nations. But rather than creating a framework for lasting peace, Lloyd George and Clemenceau focused on maintaining their own territories and punishing Germany. The resulting Treaty of Versailles included language establishing a League of Nations, but also harsh punishment for Germany. With the terms of the treaty set, Wilson campaigned across the United States to build public opinion for its terms and for the United States joining the League of Nations. But some in the United States did not want the nation to join the league. They believed doing so would allow other nations to meddle in the United States' domestic affairs. Despite a great effort, Wilson could not muster enough support for the league. The United States would not become a member of the League of Nations.

WILSON'S FOURTEEN POINTS

Wilson presented his Fourteen Points for world peace to Congress in a speech on January 8, 1918. But Wilson's audience was much larger than the members of Congress. He designed his speech to inspire the Allied forces and erode the will of Germany and its allies. Copies of the speech were dropped across enemy lines in Europe. The Fourteen Points were well received in Europe, and Germany used them as the basis for the terms of the armistice in November 1918.

Left to right: **Prime Minister David Lloyd George, Premier Vittorio Orlando, Premier Georges Clemenceau, and President Woodrow Wilson at the Paris Peace Conference on May 27, 1919**

While traveling to build support for the League of Nations, Wilson's health started failing. He suffered a stroke in the fall of 1919. Though he served out his presidential term, he never fully recovered. He died on February 3, 1924.

David Lloyd George was the first and only Welshman to serve as the British prime minister.

CHAPTER 6

PRIME MINISTER DAVID LLOYD GEORGE

David Lloyd George was the prime minister of the United Kingdom in the last two years of the war. He was born on January 17, 1863, in Manchester, England, but grew up in Wales. Lloyd George was elected to Parliament in 1890 and served for 55 years.

During his service, Lloyd George gained a reputation as a gifted debater and champion of the working class. Charming, witty, daring, and eloquent, Lloyd George was able to see the broader meaning of complex issues. However, he became notorious for his use of underhanded methods to get the results he wanted. He was also ruthless against those who opposed him and his ideas. This combination of persuasiveness, charm, and ruthlessness enabled Lloyd George to take drastic action to win the war once he became prime minister.

THE MANSION HOUSE SPEECH

One of Lloyd George's first forays into foreign affairs was his Mansion House speech in reaction to Germany's aggression toward France in Morocco. On July 21, 1911, Lloyd George spoke at the Mansion House in London, warning Germany if it forced the United Kingdom to choose between peace and war, the British would choose war. The United Kingdom, he said, must keep "her place and her prestige among the Great Powers of the world."[1]

ADVOCATING FOR WAR

In 1908, Herbert Henry Asquith was elected prime minister of the United Kingdom. He chose Lloyd George as his chancellor of the exchequer, the office responsible for setting the country's budget and fiscal policies. While serving as Exchequer, Lloyd George continued to serve in Parliament. He focused his efforts on domestic issues, leaving issues of foreign policy to his colleagues. But this changed in 1911 during the Agadir Crisis with Germany. He worked with Asquith and Asquith's foreign secretary, Sir Edward Grey, to issue a stern warning to Germany over its intimidation of France. Throughout the next decade, the United Kingdom's relationships with other nations would become Lloyd George's primary focus.

Lloyd George was serving in Parliament and as chancellor of the exchequer when Archduke Franz Ferdinand was assassinated in Sarajevo, Bosnia. As tensions grew between Serbia, Austria-Hungary, Germany, and Russia, Lloyd George advocated for staying out of any potential conflict. But the United Kingdom's alliance with France required the United Kingdom to come to France's aid. As the nations of Europe declared war on each other between July 28 and August 6, 1914, Lloyd George realized war was inevitable. He threw his full effort into managing the United Kingdom's wartime finances.

Lloyd George's primary focus was funding the rapid production of weapons, ammunition, and other military supplies. In 1915, Asquith named Lloyd George the minister of munitions, a role Lloyd George took on with enthusiasm and boundless energy. To increase production, he made an unprecedented move and invited big business leaders and leaders of the labor unions to help him in his effort to get supplies to the troops fighting in France. His tireless efforts meant British troops were well supplied for their first major battle along the Somme River in France.

But Lloyd George was not content with constricting his attention to munitions. He wanted to participate in war strategy decisions but found he often disagreed with the heads of the military, Sir William Robertson and Sir Douglas Haig. Lloyd George believed the United Kingdom must focus on the eastern front in Russia and the Middle East to win the war. But Robertson and Haig disagreed, declaring the western front most important for winning the war.

Factory laborers in Sheffield, England, work to produce munitions to help aid the war effort.

Lloyd George found himself in a position of more power on June 1916. On June 5, Secretary of State for War Sir Horatio Herbert Kitchener was drowned when a German mine sunk his ship. Asquith appointed Lloyd George as Kitchener's replacement, a position he held for five months. During that time, Robertson, the chief of the imperial general staff, curbed Lloyd George's power to make military decisions. But Lloyd George did not have to wait long to gain more influence on the direction of the war. Asquith resigned on December 5, and Lloyd George was elected prime minister on December 7, 1916.

LEADING AN EMPIRE AT WAR

In the month before he became prime minister, Lloyd George decided that to win the war, the United Kingdom had to delegate daily war decisions to a small wartime committee. Asquith's war committee had 23 members. Its slow decision-making frustrated Lloyd George, who saw it as a detriment to the war effort. His first decision as prime minister was to dismiss Asquith's large committee and replace it with a committee of just five members. Immediately, crucial military decisions were made more quickly.

One of the pressing issues facing the new prime minister was German submarine warfare. Since the start of the war in 1914, German U-boats patrolled British waters. This threatened the supply chain of the United Kingdom, an island nation. If ships could not deliver food and other supplies, the United Kingdom's war effort would be crippled and its people would starve. In February 1915, Germany declared unrestricted submarine warfare in a zone around the United Kingdom. German U-boats would attack merchant and military ships without warning, including those belonging to neutral countries and carrying citizens of neutral countries. In September, Germany stopped the policy after pressure from the United States after the sinking of the British ship *Lusitania*,

HERBERT HENRY ASQUITH

1852–1928

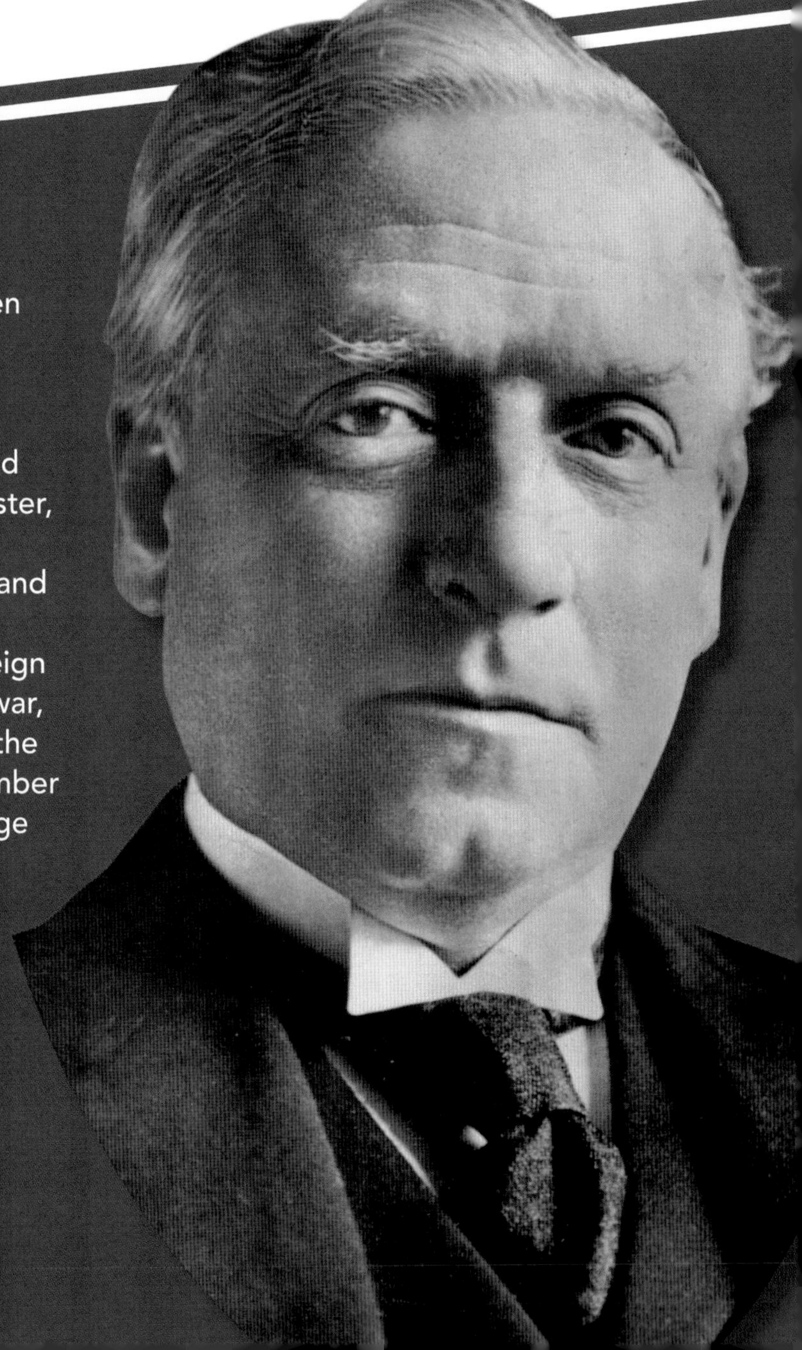

Herbert Henry Asquith served as prime minister of the United Kingdom between 1908 and 1916. He was elected to Parliament in 1886, four years before Lloyd George's own election. Similar to Lloyd George, Asquith was eloquent and supported social reform. As prime minister, Asquith's attention initially focused on domestic issues, including unrest in Ireland and the push for the vote for women. World War I forced him to focus on foreign policy issues. After a poor start to the war, Asquith struggled to build support for the war among the British people. In December 1916, Asquith resigned and Lloyd George became prime minister.

which had Americans aboard. But by February 1917, Germany announced it would resume unrestricted submarine warfare. In just three months, the U-boats sank more than 500 merchant ships.[2]

Lloyd George had to act. He urged the British navy to change how ships traveled in the war zone. Instead of moving through the zone individually, merchant ships were organized into convoys. Each convoy had a warship escort. The merchant ships were repainted to be harder to spot at sea. The changes worked. By the end of the war, U-boats no longer posed a threat to supply ships arriving and departing British ports.

Despite increased efficiency with a smaller committee and his success combating German U-boats, Lloyd George continued to butt heads with Robertson and Haig. Lloyd George had lost faith in Robertson and Haig's ability to carry out a successful strategy along the western front. Without gaining their approval or input, Lloyd George approached the leaders of France to propose unifying the

FOOD SHORTAGES AND RATIONING

The German U-boat attacks led to a food crisis in the United Kingdom. Without imports from other countries, the British people could not produce enough food to feed themselves. To combat hunger, Lloyd George instituted a food rationing system in the summer of 1918. The system assigned every person a fixed amount of certain foods each week. Each adult and child was rationed four ounces (113 g) of butter and margarine each week. Working men could purchase seven pounds (3 kg) of bread each week, while women could purchase four pounds (2 kg). Sugar and flour were also rationed. Though people ate less than they were used to during peacetime, few Britons starved during the war.

British and French troops under French command for the next offensive. This underhanded move angered Robertson and Haig, and their distrust of Lloyd George was validated when the first major offensive of the unified troops failed. In the wake of the failure, Haig urged Lloyd George to agree to launch a new offensive in the Belgian town of Passchendaele at the end of July 1917. Lloyd George was reluctant but had little ground to stand on, so he agreed to move ahead with the offensive.

PASSCHENDAELE

The third battle of Ypres, commonly called Passchendaele, was a costly conflict. Men and horses drowned in the deep mud left behind by record-setting heavy rain and widespread shelling of the area over four months. The heavy mud rendered tanks and rifles useless. By early November, the Allied forces had had enough. Haig called for an end to the offensive, having only gained five miles (8 km) of ground in four months of fighting.

But the offensive at Passchendaele was also a failure. It stopped Germany from advancing toward France, but it did not gain the Allies any ground. Lloyd George moved to replace Haig, who had predicted a conclusive victory. But instead of doing so directly and publicly, Lloyd George took measures to undermine Haig and his ally Robertson, who resigned in February 1918. He intentionally kept Haig short of troops over the winter of 1917 and 1918, nearly leading to a German victory in March 1918. Haig's near defeat was the excuse Lloyd George needed to replace him. Lloyd George's underhanded moves made it possible for the Allied forces to come under the sole command of

The muddy battle of Passchendaele cost 325,000 Allied casualties.

French Commander Ferdinand Foch. Similar to a smaller war committee, a single commander of the Allied forces made decision-making more efficient. With the streamlined command structure and the addition of American troops once the United States joined the war, the Allies gained momentum in the spring and summer of 1918, leading to Germany's surrender in November 1918.

NEGOTIATING PEACE

The war over, Lloyd George turned his attention to negotiating a permanent peace with Germany. He met French Premier Georges Clemenceau and US President Woodrow Wilson in Paris to discuss the terms of a peace treaty. Since France had suffered the most at the hands of the Germans, Clemenceau called for harsh punishment for Germany. Wilson's primary focus was establishing the League of Nations.

Lloyd George knew he needed to bridge the gap between these two leaders to find a compromise. However, British troops had also suffered greatly, and he faced pressure to side with Clemenceau. He also needed to ensure the United Kingdom would not lose any territory abroad in the agreement. When the resulting Treaty of Versailles was signed in June 1919, Lloyd George was recognized for his contributions to forging a permanent peace. King George V awarded him the Order of Merit in August 1919.

LIFE AFTER WAR

Though recognized for his work at the Paris Peace Conference, Lloyd George's reception at home was lukewarm. His underhanded actions during the war, as well as his downsizing of the war committee—and thus Parliament's influence on war strategy—did not sit well with his fellow politicians. The United Kingdom also faced unemployment and labor strikes. It nearly immediately fell into an

David Lloyd George signed the Treaty of Versailles on June 28, 1919.

armed conflict over Ireland's independence, which lasted until 1921. Lloyd George negotiated the end of the conflict, creating the Irish Free State.

Then, in 1922, allegations spread about Lloyd George, claiming he had sold knighthoods and other honors. Later that year, Lloyd George's remaining political supporters criticized his foreign policy in Turkey, which had broken up from the Ottoman Empire, believing he meant to go to war with the country. Without their support, Lloyd George was forced to resign as prime minister on October 19, 1922. He continued to serve in Parliament until 1945. He died the same year on March 26 in Wales.

Clemenceau lived in the United States before forming an alliance with the nation during World War I.

CHAPTER 7

PREMIER GEORGES CLEMENCEAU

Georges Clemenceau was the premier of France in the last year of World War I. He was born on September 28, 1841, in the coastal town of Vendée. Clemenceau was strongly opinionated when it came to government issues and was jailed for a time during the reign of Napoleon III for his revolutionary actions. After he was released, Clemenceau moved to the United States. He worked there as a teacher and journalist before returning to France in 1869. Once back, Clemenceau began a career of public service, punctuated by time as a journalist.

After serving as the mayor of Montmartre and in the lower house of France's Parliament, Clemenceau was elected to the

French Senate in 1902. He became interior minister and then premier in 1906. During his time as the leader of the French government, Clemenceau helped expand the military. He believed France needed a strong army of French citizens to defend the country if it was ever invaded. During his tenure, he helped solidify the alliance between France and the United Kingdom. He also led France when it came to a shaky agreement with Germany over Morocco in 1909. But that same year, he resigned after a disagreement with French statesman Théophile Delcassé, who had helped build France's alliances with other European countries.

After he left the government, Clemenceau traveled to South America.

Throughout his life, Clemenceau was a writer.

There, he gave speeches on the virtues of democracy. "It is the only form of government which can establish equality for all, and which can bring closer the ultimate goals: freedom and justice," he declared.[1] Just two years later, Clemenceau was elected to the French Senate once again. After Germany's actions in Morocco in 1911, Clemenceau was convinced the country meant to go to war. He did not want France to be caught unprepared, so he used his power in the Senate to urge the government to strengthen its military. He made his views public by starting his own newspaper, *L'Homme Libre* (The Freeman) in 1913.

A year later, France was at war with Germany and its allies. Clemenceau continued to serve in the Senate but found his newspaper and his opinions censored and then suppressed once fighting began. Undeterred, he started a new paper, *L'Homme Enchaîné* (The Chained Man). Though censors continued to cut writing from the paper, it was not shut down. Clemenceau continued to use his paper to

THE BATTLE OF CHEMIN DES DAMES

On April 16, 1917, 1.2 million French soldiers began fighting in what became a catastrophic defeat for France. At least 30,000 soldiers died in the first ten days of the battle of Chemin des Dames, and after a month of fighting, the men had had enough. Approximately 40,000 men mutinied, refusing to carry on fighting. By September, the French government had made improvements to the soldiers' living conditions and increased how often they were allowed to take leave. The government took 3,400 mutineers to court for their actions and sentenced more than 550 to death, though historians believe only 50 were eventually executed.[2]

call for a stronger military. He demanded France provide more guns, munitions, and better medical service for its soldiers.

THE TIGER ROUSES FRANCE

Three years into the war, morale was low in France and supplies for the military and people at home were scarce. French President Raymond Poincaré knew it was time for a change. As president, Poincaré was responsible for choosing the premier, who ran the daily operations of the government. He asked Clemenceau to lead the country as premier once again. Though not an admirer of Clemenceau, Poincaré realized Clemenceau, a staunch supporter of the war and France's war effort, was the person to lead France to victory.

In November 1917, Clemenceau accepted. By this time, Clemenceau had earned the nickname "the Tiger" for his dogged defense of France and its interests. He made the "will to victory" the theme of his government. In the early years of the war, Clemenceau had worked to convince US President Woodrow Wilson to enter the war on the side of France. When the United States finally joined the war in 1917, Clemenceau was overjoyed. The influx of US troops helped improve morale among French troops.

Clemenceau's first action as premier was to also name himself minister of war. He focused the French government solely on winning the war; he pursued no other interests. This singular focus of his government left no room for people who disagreed with his tactics or with France's involvement in the war. He believed the Allied forces would be more successful if they were unified under one commander. Since the start of the war, nations had controlled their own militaries. This made it difficult to coordinate attacks. In addition, sometimes the military leaders disagreed, making it difficult for troops to take action. By March 1918, Clemenceau had convinced France's allies one commander would help the Allies win the war. French Commander Ferdinand Foch took control of the Allied forces in the spring of 1918. Though the Germans still posed a formidable threat, the Allies gained momentum under Foch.

THE PARIS PEACE CONFERENCE

When Germany signed the armistice that ended World War I, Clemenceau broke down in tears. But though the war was over, Clemenceau still faced a stiff challenge. He had to negotiate with the United Kingdom and the United

FERDINAND FOCH

By the time he was named commander of the unified Allied forces, Ferdinand Foch had already proven himself a wise military leader numerous times in the war. The former French commander in chief, Joseph Joffre, relied on Foch to coordinate the attacks of the French, Belgian, and British forces in major battles in the Belgian towns of Ypres and Yser. Foch was finally recognized for his efforts in May 1917, when he was appointed adviser to the Allied forces. But as adviser, he could not control troops. He urged Allied political leaders to create a single command for the Allied militaries. It took Clemenceau and British Prime Minister David Lloyd George nearly a year to realize Foch was right. By then, the clear choice for commander was Foch himself. Between April and October 1918, Foch led the Allied forces to beat back the Germans in two major offensives, forcing Germany to ask for an end to fighting.

Clemenceau reviews US soldiers after their arrival in France in 1917.

States to create a peace agreement that would meet the approval of the French people. Many in France wanted Germany to pay for their aggression. Though negotiations were kept civil, Clemenceau personally disliked the leaders of the United States and the United Kingdom, Woodrow Wilson especially. Wilson, he thought, was too idealistic, ignoring the real harm Germany had caused in favor of his idea of world peace.

Despite their differences, the three leaders were able to come to a consensus. Clemenceau campaigned hard to disarm Germany and force the country to repay France for its aggression with money and territory, including the region of Alsace-Lorraine that rests between France and Germany. He negotiated a buffer between France and Germany by stationing Allied forces in the German Rhineland in western Germany for 15 years. He also negotiated stronger treaties with the United States and the United Kingdom in the hope of ensuring peace.

Though many of his demands were met, Clemenceau still believed the final treaty was too lenient. He did get one final jab at Germany, however. He negotiated the signing of the treaty in the Hall of Mirrors at the Palace of Versailles. It was the same hall where Germany was declared a country and Kaiser Wilhelm I was proclaimed its emperor.

AISNE

Clemenceau remained determined to win the war even when French troops suffered defeats on the battlefield. The third battle of the Aisne started with disaster for French and Allied troops. Early on May 27, 1918, German troops advanced nine miles (15 km) behind Allied lines near the Aisne River in northwest France. The attack took French troops by surprise. In a matter of hours, the Germans broke through four French divisions and four British ones. By the end of the day, the Germans had created a wedge 25 miles (40 km) wide in the French line along the western front. Three days later, the Germans had taken 50,000 Allied soldiers prisoners and captured 800 Allied weapons.[3]

After the disastrous first day of the battle, Clemenceau urged Foch to regroup French forces along the Aisne River. It took French troops a few days to regroup, but by June 1, the French forces were able to stop the German advance. The Germans had driven 30 miles (48 km) farther into France, and the Allied forces had suffered 123,000 casualties.[4] It had been France's worst defeat in the war. But Clemenceau's determination to win and quick and decisive leadership kept Germany from reaching Paris and dealing a blow to French morale.

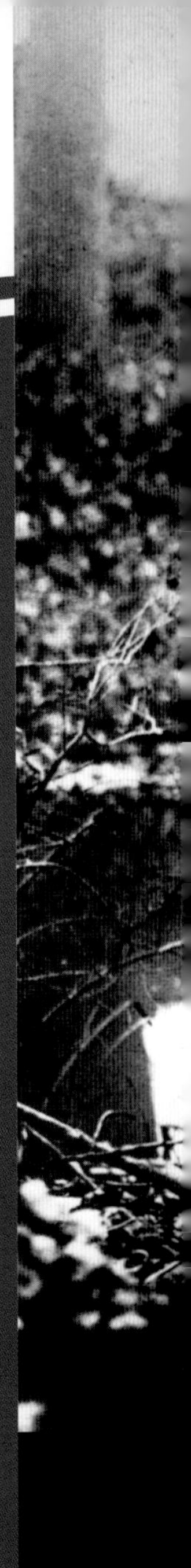

German soldiers cross the Aisne River and prepare to battle the French.

Clemenceau signs the Treaty of Versailles in the Hall of Mirrors.

AFTER THE WAR

Once the Paris Peace Conference concluded in 1919, French politics turned against Clemenceau. Now that the war was over, people started to criticize his one-man control of the French government during the war. They also believed he did not negotiate harsh enough terms for Germany at the Paris Peace Conference. Defeated in the election of 1920, Clemenceau stepped down from the premiership and left politics.

THE HALL OF MIRRORS

The Hall of Mirrors in the Palace of Versailles is an imposing room. It is 240 feet (73 m) long and 35 feet (11 m) wide. Seventeen arches along the interior wall each contain 21 mirrors that reflect views of the gardens through the opposite windows. It is also where Chancellor Bismarck announced the separate German states would be united as one country. It was for this reason Clemenceau wished to hold the signing of the Treaty of Versailles in the Hall of Mirrors. He believed signing terms of its defeat in the room where it had declared its nationhood would further humiliate Germany.

After spending some time traveling, Clemenceau retired to Vendée and wrote his memoirs, including *In the Evening of My Thought*, which included his philosophical beliefs. He died on November 26, 1929, in Paris.

Crowds in New York gathered to celebrate the end of World War I on Peace Monday, November 11, 1918.

CHAPTER 8

THE ELEVENTH HOUR

By October 1918, Germany's military was exhausted and the country could no longer fight. Austria-Hungary also lay defeated at the hands of the Allies. In the first week of October, Germany sued for peace. Commander Foch, representatives from the German military, and the German secretary of state met on November 11, 1918, to discuss terms of an armistice.

The armistice called for an end to fighting within six hours of its signing. Germany was instructed to immediately leave Belgium, France, Luxemburg, and the region of Alsace-Lorraine. It also agreed to leave the left bank of the Rhine River, where a neutral area was established. During the retreat, Germany was prohibited from harming inhabitants in the cities and towns they passed through. They could not destroy cropland or take supplies

GLOBAL PEACE IN A RAILROAD CAR

The armistice that ended World War I was not signed in a great hall. Instead, Foch met representatives of Germany in his personal railway car. The car was stationed in Rethondes, a town in northern France. The document was signed at 5:00 a.m. the morning of November 11, 1918. But the armistice did not go into effect until 11:00 a.m.—the eleventh hour of the eleventh day of the eleventh month.

and food as they went. They had to leave railways, roads, bridges, and other infrastructure intact. Additionally, they gave up thousands of artillery guns and machine guns, 1,700 airplanes, 5,000 train locomotives, and 150,000 wagons.[1]

Germany also gave up any land gains it made during the war, resetting its boundaries to where they lay before the war in August 1914. It also lost its territory in Africa. Peace agreements between Germany and Austria-Hungary were also voided. Germany had 30 days to comply with the terms of the armistice; only then would a formal peace treaty follow.

A COSTLY WAR

The number of troops mobilized, killed, and wounded in World War I was unlike anything any of the major leaders had experienced before. Partly due to heavy losses, Russia had withdrawn from the war in December 1917, nearly a year before the signing of the armistice. Under Nicholas II, it had mobilized the most troops—12 million soldiers—and suffered the most casualties of any force in the war, despite its early exit from the conflict. Under Wilhelm II, Germany had mobilized 11 million troops and suffered 7.1 million casualties.[2]

Germany and her allies had mobilized 22.9 million troops. More than 3 million of them lost their lives in the conflict, and 8.4 million were wounded. The Allies had mobilized 42.2 million troops. More than 5 million of them lost their lives, and 12.8 million were wounded. In total, the war had cost 8.5 million lives, and 57.5 percent of all troops were either killed, wounded, taken prisoner, or went missing.[3]

Foch, *second from right*, and other Allied representatives outside Foch's railway carriage

CHANGING BORDERS

1914

1921

After World War I ended in 1918, smaller wars continued in eastern Europe. By 1921, European borders were relatively stable and remained in place until World War II began in the late 1930s.

Mass graves were dug to bury the millions of soldiers lost.

MILITARY CONFLICT BRINGS POLITICAL CHANGE

World War I had a profound effect on many European governments. At the outbreak of the war, only France was a republic; all other nations were monarchies. In 1917, another republic, the United States, entered the war.

The same year, Czar Nicholas II of Russia abdicated the throne. The monarchy toppled, and the socialist Bolsheviks took control in Russia. On July 17, 1918, Nicholas and his entire family were executed. After a period of civil war between 1919 and 1922, Russia became the Union of Soviet Socialist Republics, or USSR. The Soviet party controlled the country until its dissolution in 1991.

Germany experienced similar upheaval. On November 3, 1918, members of the nation's navy revolted, and unrest spread to other branches of the military and workers at home. Two days before the signing of the armistice, Kaiser Wilhelm II fled for the Netherlands. He never returned to Germany. The day Wilhelm fled, a new government called the Weimar Republic was declared. This new republic had a tenuous hold on the government of Germany, and many radical political groups arose in the 1920s and 1930s. One of these, the Nazi Party, led by Adolf Hitler, would play a large role in rebuilding Germany's military power and its aggression in the late 1930s, leading to World War II.

THE WEIMAR REPUBLIC

The Weimar Republic lasted for 12 years and was bookended between the old monarchy, led by Kaiser Wilhelm II, and a new dictatorship, led by Adolf Hitler. Though Wilhelm had brought Germany into World War I, at the end of the war, the German public placed blame on Germany's political parties. Many believed the parties were responsible for Germany's defeat and the demoralizing terms of the Treaty of Versailles. This distrust of the government and its general weakness allowed the Nazi Party to gain popularity throughout the 1920s and 1930s.

After its defeat at the hands of the Italians at the Piave River in spring 1918, the Austro-Hungarian Empire also fell. Throughout the war, the empire had done a poor job supplying troops, and unrest at the front and at home grew until the monarchy was overthrown in October 1918. A republic was established, and in the years following the war, the independent nations of Austria and Hungary were created.

THE TREATY OF VERSAILLES

French President Georges Clemenceau, British Prime Minister David Lloyd George, and US President Woodrow Wilson presented the terms of the Treaty of Versailles to Germany in 1919 in the Hall of Mirrors in the Versailles Palace in France. Wilson hoped to draft a treaty that created permanent peace. But Clemenceau and Lloyd George were more interested in maintaining or expanding their empires and issuing harsh punishment to Germany.

While Clemenceau and Lloyd George were criticized for not punishing Germany enough, to the Germans, the treaty was considered a *Diktat*, or "dictated peace." The new government in Germany tried to change or defy the treaty's terms in the 1920s and 1930s. The treaty also gave radical groups a rallying point. Hitler and his Nazi Party gained popularity as they promised to rebuild Germany's military and bring Germany back to greatness. The Nazis appealed to growing German sentiment that the leaders of the Weimar Republic sold Germany out when it agreed to the terms of the treaty. The unstable rule of the Weimar Republic created an opportunity for Hitler to seize power and lead the country into another disastrous conflict, World War II.

HITLER'S SERVICE IN WORLD WAR I

Future German dictator Adolf Hitler served in the German army during World War I. He was wounded twice, promoted to the rank of corporal, and awarded medals for his service. It was along the front lines where he started to believe the anti-Semitic ideas that were permeating the German military. The end of the war created a crisis for Hitler, who had found purpose in serving in the military. After the war, the German army hired Hitler to spy on the German Workers' Party, which would become his introduction to politics.

TIMELINE

1882

Germany, Austria-Hungary, and Italy sign the Triple Alliance.

1888

Wilhelm II becomes emperor of Germany.

1894

Nicholas II becomes czar of Russia; France and Russia secretly sign the Dual Alliance.

1900

Victor Emmanuel III becomes king of Italy; France and Italy enter into a secret alliance.

July 28, 1914

Austria-Hungary declares war against Serbia, starting World War I.

August 14, 1914

The battle of the Frontiers begins.

May 7, 1915

A German U-boat sinks the *Lusitania*.

December 7, 1916

David Lloyd George becomes the prime minister of the United Kingdom.

1908
Austria-Hungary annexes Bosnia.

1909
Italy breaks the Triple Alliance and signs a secret agreement with Russia.

1912
Woodrow Wilson is elected president of the United States.

June 28, 1914
Serbian Gavrilo Princip assassinates Austro-Hungarian Archduke Franz Ferdinand.

April 6, 1917
The United States enters World War I.

November 1917
Georges Clemenceau becomes premier of France.

November 11, 1918
Germany signs an armistice ending the fighting in Europe.

June 1919
Germany and the Allies sign the Treaty of Versailles, formally ending the war.

ESSENTIAL FACTS

KEY PLAYERS

- Wilhelm II was the emperor of Germany.
- Nicholas II was the czar of Russia.
- Georges Clemenceau was the premier of France in the last year of the war.
- David Lloyd George was the prime minister of the United Kingdom in the last years of the war.
- Victor Emmanuel III was the king of Italy.
- Woodrow Wilson was the president of the United States.

KEY STATISTICS

- Together, the Allies mobilized 42.2 million troops.
- Russia mobilized 12 million soldiers, more than any other nation.
- Under Wilhelm II, Germany mobilized 11 million troops.
- Approximately 8.5 million soldiers lost their lives in World War I.

KEY ALLIANCES

- Germany, Austria-Hungary, and Italy were allies under the Triple Alliance of 1882.
- France and Russia were allies under the Dual Alliance of 1894.
- Italy changed alliances in 1909, signing a secret agreement with Russia.

IMPACT ON THE WAR

The leaders of the major European powers were responsible for leading their nations to war in 1914. Wilhelm II's aggressive, bombastic nature made him unpredictable to other leaders, while Nicholas II's cautiousness made him an unassertive ruler. Clemenceau, Lloyd George, and Wilson were able to see past their differences during the Paris Peace Conference.

QUOTES

"It would be the irony of fate if my administration had to deal chiefly with foreign affairs."

—Woodrow Wilson

"I look upon the people and the nation, as handed on to me, as [a] responsibility conferred upon me by God. And I believe, as it is written in the Bible, that it is my duty to increase this heritage, for which one day I shall be called upon to give an account. Whoever tries to interfere with my task, I shall crush."

—Kaiser Wilhelm II

GLOSSARY

ABDICATE
To give up power or office.

ANARCHIST
A person who believes countries should not have governments.

ANNEX
To add to one's territory to make one's country larger.

ARMISTICE
A temporary stop of fighting by mutual agreement.

CENSOR
Something examined and changed to delete information the government finds objectionable.

CONVOY
A group that travels together for protection.

FASCISM
A political system in which the government controls the economy and no opposing political parties are permitted.

FRONT
An area where a battle is taking place.

MOBILIZE
To become prepared for war.

MUNITION
War supplies.

NATIONALIST
Someone who supports his or her nation above all others.

NEUTRAL
To not favor either side in a conflict, such as a war.

OFFENSIVE
Large-scale attack against the enemy.

PARLIAMENT
The supreme legislative body of a country.

PROPAGANDA
Information used to support a political group or point of view, or to persuade the audience to support their country's participation in a war.

ADDITIONAL RESOURCES

SELECTED BIBLIOGRAPHY

Berg, A. Scott. *Wilson*. New York: Putnam, 2013. Print.

Clark, Christopher M. *The Sleepwalkers: How Europe Went to War in 1914*. New York: HarperCollins, 2013. Print.

"Personalities of the Big Three: Woodrow Wilson, Georges Clemenceau and David Lloyd George." University of Virginia, n.d. Web. 29 Apr. 2015.

"Wilhelm II (1859–1941)." *History*. BBC, 2014. Web. 20 Apr. 2015.

"World War I Aftermath." *Holocaust Encyclopedia*. United States Holocaust Memorial Museum, 20 June 2014. Web. 12 May 2015.

FURTHER READINGS

Fleming, Candace. *The Family Romanov: Murder, Rebellion, and the Fall of Imperial Russia*. New York: Schwartz & Wade, 2014. Print.

Frith, Margaret. *Who Was Woodrow Wilson?* New York: Grosset and Dunlap, 2015. Print.

Kenney, Karen Latchana. *Everything World War I*. Washington, DC: National Geographic Society, 2014. Print.

WEBSITES

To learn more about Essential Library of World War I, visit **booklinks.abdopublishing.com**. These links are routinely monitored and updated to provide the most current information available.

PLACES TO VISIT

National World War I Museum
100 W. Twenty-Sixth Street
Kansas City, MO 64108
816-888-8100
https://theworldwar.org
Exhibits and educational programs explore the history of World War I and share stories through the eyes of those who lived it. The museum is attached to the Liberty Memorial, a monument to those who served.

The Woodrow Wilson Presidential Library & Museum
20 N. Coalter Street
Staunton, VA 24401
540-885-0897
http://www.woodrowwilson.org
View materials about Wilson, including memoirs of people who worked with him.

SOURCE NOTES

CHAPTER 1. SLOUCHING TOWARD WAR

1. Margaret McMillan. "The Rhyme of History: Lessons of the Great War." *The Brookings Essay*. The Brookings Institution, 14 Dec. 2013. Web. 5 June 2015.

2. "Eastern Front Strategy 1914: World War I." *Encyclopædia Britannica*. Encyclopædia Britannica Inc., 2015. Web. 27 Apr. 2015.

3. "The Battle of Verdun." *The Great War*. PBS, n.d. Web. 26 Apr. 2015.

4. Ibid.

CHAPTER 2. KAISER WILHELM II

1. Christopher M. Clark. *The Sleepwalkers: How Europe Went to War in 1914*. New York: HarperCollins, 2013. Print. 520.

2. Ibid. 522.

3. "The German Army Marches Through Brussels, 1914." *EyeWitness to History*. Ibis Communications, n.d. Web. 27 Apr. 2015.

CHAPTER 3. CZAR NICHOLAS II

1. "February Revolution Begins in Russia." *History*. A+E Television Networks, n.d. Web. 6 May 2015.

CHAPTER 4. KING VICTOR EMMANUEL III

1. Christopher M. Clark. *The Sleepwalkers: How Europe Went to War in 1914*. New York: HarperCollins, 2013. Print. 244.

2. "Italy Declares War on Austria-Hungary." *History*. A+E Television Networks, 23 May 2014. Web. 22 Apr. 2015.

3. "Pope Benedict XV Named to Papacy." *History*. A+E Television Networks, 3 Sept. 2013. Web. 10 May 2015.

4. "Battle of Caporetto." *Encyclopædia Britannica*. Encyclopædia Britannica Inc., 2015. Web. 10 May 2015.

5. Michael Duffy. "Battles–The Battle of Vittorio Veneto, 1918." *First World War*. First World War, 22 Aug. 2009. Web. 10 May 2015.

CHAPTER 5. PRESIDENT WOODROW WILSON

1. H.W Brands. *Woodrow Wilson*. New York: Henry Holt, 2003. Print. 42.

2. "Germany Resumes Unrestricted Submarine Warfare." *History*. A+E Television Networks, 1 Feb. 2015. Web. 11 May 2015.

3. A. Scott Berg. *Wilson*. New York: Putnam, 2013. Print. 440.

4. Ibid. 358–359.

5. "WWI Casualty and Death Tables." *PBS*. PBS, n.d. Web. 27 Apr. 2015.

6. A. Scott Berg. *Wilson*. New York: Putnam, 2013. Print. 476.

7. Ibid. 473.

SOURCE NOTES CONTINUED

CHAPTER 6. PRIME MINISTER DAVID LLOYD GEORGE

1. Christopher M. Clark. *The Sleepwalkers: How Europe Went to War in 1914*. New York: HarperCollins, 2013. Print. 209–210.

2. Jessica Talarico. "The U-Boat Campaign That Almost Broke Britain." *Imperial War Museums*. Imperial War Museums, 2014. Web. 23 Mar. 2015.

CHAPTER 7. PREMIER GEORGES CLEMENCEAU

1. "Georges Clemenceau." *Encyclopædia Britannica*. Encyclopædia Britannica Inc., 2015. Web. 22 Apr. 2015.

2. Rick Smith. "France Commemorates a Dark Chapter in World War I History." *New York Times*. New York Times Company, 15 Apr. 2007. Web. 27 Apr. 2015.

3. Michael Duffy. "Battles–The Battle of Vittorio Veneto, 1918." *First World War*. First World War, 22 Aug. 2009. Web. 10 May 2015.

4. Spencer C. Tucker and Priscilla Mary Roberts. *World War I: A Student Encyclopedia*. Santa Barbara, CA: ABC-CLIO, 2006. Web. 7 May 2015. 109–110.

CHAPTER 8. THE ELEVENTH HOUR

1. "Terms of Armistice with Germany." *National Archives*. National Archives, n.d. Web. 9 Apr. 2015.

2. "WWI Casualty and Death Tables." *PBS*. PBS, n.d. Web. 27 Apr. 2015.

3. Ibid.

INDEX

Agadir Crisis, 42, 66
Alexandra, 29–30, 35–36
Allied forces, 13, 62, 72, 73, 81, 83, 84
Alps, 45–46, 47, 49
armistice, 13, 26, 38, 62, 81, 89, 90, 95
Asquith, Herbert Henry, 66–70
Austria-Hungary, 5–8, 15, 16, 19–21, 31–35, 38, 43–45, 47, 49, 54, 60, 67, 89, 90

Balkans, 5, 7, 20, 31, 32, 42–43, 44
battles
    Aisne, third battle of, 84
    Caporetto, 47, 48
    Chemin des Dames, 79
    Frontiers, the, 10
    Passchendaele, 72
    Somme, the, 12
    Verdun, 12
    Vittorio Veneto, 48, 49
    Ypres, third battle of, 72
Belgium, 8, 10, 23–24, 60, 89
Benedict XV, 45
Bismarck, Otto von, 16, 87
Bolsheviks, 13, 37–38, 39, 95
Bosnia, 5–7, 32–33, 66
Bulgaria, 38

Cadorna, Luigi, 47, 48
Caprivi, Leo von, 16
casualties, 12, 35, 84, 90–91
Clemenceau, Georges, 13, 62, 74, 77–87, 96
Committee on Public Information, US, 59
Congress, US, 13, 56–59, 62
Council of National Defense, 59
credits, US, 55–56
Cyrenaica, 42

Diaz, Armando, 47, 48, 49
draft, 58–59
Dual Alliance, 16, 31–33

eastern front, 47, 67
exile, 26, 36, 39

Falkenhayn, Erich von, 22, 24–26
Foch, Ferdinand, 13, 47, 49, 73, 81, 84, 89, 90
food rationing, 59, 71
Fourteen Points, 62
France, 6, 8, 10–11, 12–13, 16, 18, 22–24, 26, 31–33, 34, 42, 44, 49, 54–56, 60, 66–67, 71–72, 74, 77–87, 89, 90, 94, 96
Franz Ferdinand, 7, 19, 20, 33, 66

George, David Lloyd, 12, 62, 65–75, 81, 96
George V, 6, 7, 8, 23, 74
Germany, 5–11, 12, 13, 15–26, 29, 31–34, 36, 38, 42, 43, 44, 49, 54, 56–57, 62, 66–67, 69, 71, 72–74, 78–79, 81, 83, 84, 87, 89–91, 95, 96–97

Haig, Douglas, 67, 71–72
Hall of Mirrors, 83, 87, 96
Hindenburg, Paul von, 24–26
Hitler, Adolf, 24, 95, 96–97
Hollweg, Bethmann, 22

Irish Free State, 75
Italo-Turkish War, 42–43, 48
Italy, 8, 41–49

Japan, 31, 33
jingoes, 57
Joseph, Franz, 8, 19, 20

Kitchener, Horatio Herbert, 68
Korea, 31

League of Nations, 61–63, 74
Lenin, Vladimir, 37, 39
L'Homme Enchaîné, 79
L'Homme Libre, 79
London, Treaty of, 45
Lusitania, 56, 57, 69

Manchuria, 31
merchant ships, 54, 56, 57, 71
Mexico, 57
Middle East, 18, 67
mobilization, 23, 33–34
Moltke, Helmuth von, 22, 23, 24
Monroe Doctrine, 52
Morgan, J. P., 54–55
Mussolini, Benito, 49

Nazi Party, 24, 95, 96
neutrality, 8, 10, 13, 22, 23–24, 44–45, 54, 56–57, 69, 89
Nicholas II, 5–7, 13, 20, 29–37, 44, 90, 95

October Manifesto, 31
Order of Merit, 74
Ottoman Empire, 33, 38, 42, 60, 75

Panther, 42
Paris, France, 10, 11, 74, 84, 87
Paris Peace Conference, 45, 62, 74, 87
Piave River, 47, 49, 96
Poincaré, Raymond, 80
Princip, Gavrilo, 8

Rasputin, 30, 35, 36
Robertson, William, 67–68, 71–72
Roosevelt, Theodore, 52, 57
Russia, 5–8, 13, 15, 16, 19, 20, 22, 23, 26, 29–39, 44, 47, 60, 67, 90, 95
Russian Revolution, 36, 38

Saint Petersburg, Russia, 29, 31, 35, 36
Selective Service Act, 58
Serbia, 5–8, 19, 20, 21, 22, 32–33, 43, 54, 60, 67
Soviets, 36–38, 39, 95
Spanish-American War, 57
State of Imminent Danger of War, 22, 34
submarine warfare, 12, 56, 57, 69, 71

Taft, Howard, 52
Triple Alliance, 43–44
Tripolitania, 42
Turkey, 75

U-boats, 56, 69, 71
Union of Soviet Socialist Republics, 95
United Kingdom, 6, 7, 8, 10, 12–13, 15, 18, 22–24, 26, 54, 56, 60, 65–71, 74, 78, 81, 83
United States, 10, 13, 18, 52–62, 69, 73, 77, 80, 83, 94

Versailles, Treaty of, 62, 74, 83, 87, 95, 96
Victor Emmanuel III, 8, 41–49

war bonds, 60
weapons, 55, 67, 84
Weimar Republic, 95, 96–97
western front, 24, 26, 45, 67, 71, 84
Wilhelm II, 5, 7, 8, 13, 15–26, 34, 42, 83, 91, 95
Wilson, Woodrow, 10, 13, 51–63, 74, 80, 83, 96
World War II, 26, 49, 95, 97

ABOUT THE AUTHOR

Amanda Lanser is a freelance writer who lives in Minneapolis, Minnesota. Amanda finds World War I fascinating. She is the author of books on a variety of topics, from Pope Francis and climate change to boa constrictors and Ötzi the Iceman. She enjoys writing for kids of all ages